MW00904532

MOMMY AND ME
COLORING BOOK

COPYRIGHT © 2024 BY SHARON ANDERSON

All rights reserved. This book or any portion thereof may not be reproduced or used in any manner whatsoever without the express written permission of the publisher except for the use of brief quotations in a book review.

THIS BOOK BELONGS TO:

_____

&

_____

WELCOME

Welcome to this Mommy and Me Coloring Book for Kids Ages 1-4!

Inside this book, you'll find a world of charming animals and their families, just waiting for your creative touch.

Grab your crayons, cozy up with your little one, and get ready to dive into a magical coloring journey together.

Each page is a new opportunity to explore colors, share smiles, and make heartwarming memories. So, let's spread out the coloring sheets and make today colorful!

Happy coloring!

THANK YOU FOR YOUR PURCHASE

Thank you so much for purchasing this coloring book. Your support means the world to self-published authors like me.

It's my hope that this coloring book brings endless fun and learning opportunities to you and your little one

Thanks again for being a part of this journey, and happy coloring!

SHARON ANDERSON

Made in the USA
Monee, IL
02 December 2024

72147063R00031